Have A Great Imagination!
Nila J. Webster

The Mystery of the Hidden Room

story by Nila J. Webster

artwork by George M. Ulrich

with special appearance by jani johe webster

Text copyright © 2014 by Nila J. Webster
Illustration copyright © 2014 by George M. Ulrich
Cover Illustration by George M. Ulrich
Book design by Craig Grant and CraigGrantCreative
craiggrant@comcast.net
All rights reserved.
Library of Congress Control Number: 2014939244
ISBN: 978-0-9618292-92
StarMist Books
Printed in China

Notes to the reader:

Welcome to the special edition of *The Mystery of the Hidden Room*,
a true story of magic and wonder beyond our wildest dreams. Before
opening the door to the magical portal, we invite you to engage in a
creative process that includes the following:

1. Find a blank sheet of paper and some colored pencils, crayons, or
   markers. If you don't have paper and crayons handy, simply close your
   eyes and imagine.

2. Imagine a magical place where all your dreams can come true.
   What kind of place would this be?
   What would happen there?
   What kind of magical creatures and beings would you meet?

3. Take the blank sheet of paper, and fill this paper with the sparkling
   colors of your own wonderful, one-of-a-kind imagination. Let your
   thoughts, ideas and visions stream onto the page, or onto the canvas
   in your mind.

4. Place this amazingly unique work of art some place special where you
   can behold it, celebrate it, and be proud of what you have created.

In your magical place are many beautiful treasures, waiting to be
discovered. We believe in you. The world needs your gifts. Send out
your sparkles, your love and your light to the whole wide universe, and
you will see. And remember, you have a very special place within you,
a place to which you can return again and again to connect with the
shimmering radiant sky-jewels of your own soul.

Check out our videos on YouTube by searching
The Story of the Hidden Room
The Gift of You, The Gift of Me

And visit our website at wherethepoemsdance.com

We look forward to seeing you there.

For my beloved Mother
jani johe webster

because we dreamed it
it came true

Table of Contents

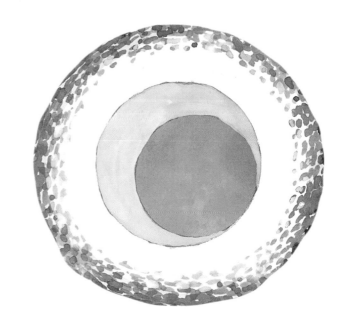

Once upon a time, when I was very young, I was sitting alone in my bedroom. In this room, all the colors of the rainbow usually laughed and danced. But on this day, I couldn't see the dancing or hear the laughter, because I was worried about what had happened at school. Some of the older students had been unkind, and I didn't know what to do about it.

What could I do?

I stared out of my bedroom window into the gray of the snowy day.

And then came a knock at the door, and in came my mother. "Today," she said, "we're going on a very special trip." I felt my heart skip a beat. My mother smiled. "We're going to a magical kingdom where all your dreams can come true. When you leave this special place, you'll leave having made the best of friends from all around the whole world. This is a place you'll want to go back to, again and again and again."

Where was the magical place?

Could it be the greatest amusement park in the whole world?

Could it be Disney World, or Six Flags, or Water Country?

Could it be Bonkers, or Chuck E. Cheese, or the Sea Breeze Amusement Park, with a

rickety roller coaster called the Jack Rabbit?

Maybe it was a place where they made all different flavors of ice cream, like Cherry

Garcia and Chunky Monkey and Chubby Hubby.

Or maybe it was a special zoo, where you can pet the animals, even the llamas and

the giraffes and the baby sheep.

As we drove downtown, I thought of a warm beach that was sunshine yellow and shimmering blue. And maybe there would be kids from all over the world, just like my mother had said, and maybe these kids could be my friends.

My mother parked the car in front of a building so big, it looked like a castle. We got out of the car and walked up what felt like a hundred steps to the huge front door. When finally we stepped inside, there was a beautiful and serene stillness, the likes of which I had never known.

I realized that we were in the library and I felt a slight disappointment.

What is a library, compared to an amusement park or a chocolate factory?

But then we walked up the stairs to the children's reading room.

In this room, brightly colored on this day of gray, the books seemed

to smile and wave, beckoning us to come in.

We came to spend many afternoons in this room. Whenever we would open a book,
It seemed that rainbows would stream out from the pages. My mother told me that
some books were so magical that when we opened the cover, we could actually walk
inside the book and talk to the characters.

We kept our ritual of going to the library. Then one day, Winter rose up from his ice cold throne, and greeted Spring, who came floating in on a warm cloud surrounded by a spray of gossamer colors.

On this magnificent of days, the librarian of the children's reading room came over to us with a radiant smile. "You know, I see you two here every week. Because I see how much you both love reading, I want to share with you a secret."

My mother had told me that librarians are special people, because they live so close to books, just as gardeners are special because they live so close to the earth, and astronomers are special because they live so close to the stars, even though the stars seem far away. What could be the secret of this librarian?

The librarian said, "In this children's reading room there is a hidden room."

Well.

I looked around the room, and saw only walls lined with colorful books. I may have been young, but no one was going to hoodwink me. And so I said, with a sad smile, "I know there's not really a hidden room."

But then my mother spoke, and her voice was filled with wonder. "Now wait a moment! We're in a library. We're surrounded by books. All our dreams can come true. Let's just see about this hidden room."

And so we followed the librarian over to a wall near a corner. There were only shelves of books. I shook my head. How could there be a hidden room behind a shelf of books?

Even so, I could not help but feel a tiny gathering of excitement as the librarian pushed a little button. Very slowly, the wall of books moved slightly to the side. I held my breath in disbelief and looked, and suddenly I saw a winding passageway leading to a closed door.

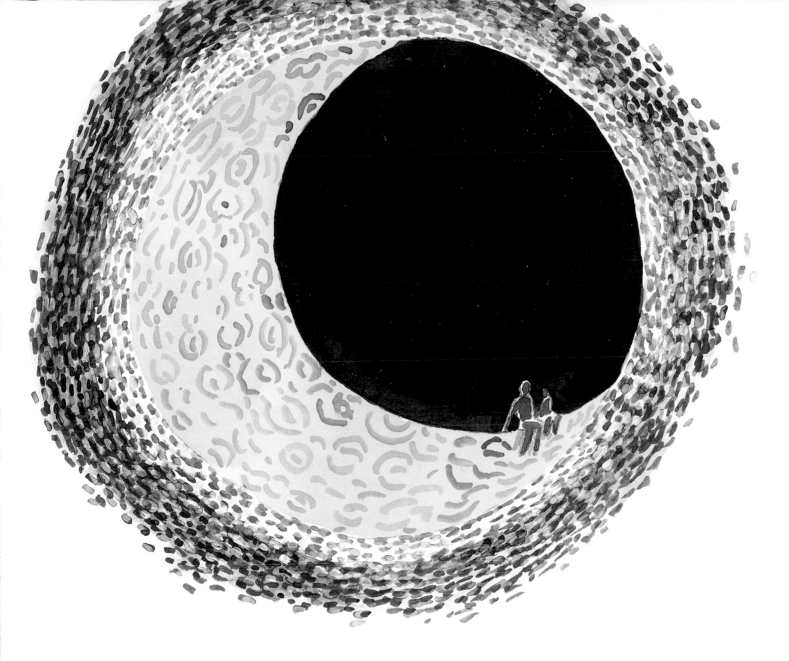

What could be in that hidden room?

Could it be something fantastic and impossible that could never happen in the real world? Could there be a magical quill that wrote magical stories about queens and kings and noble knights?

Could there be a time machine?

Could there be an enchanted forest where the animals and the trees could talk to you? Could there be a place where on the darkest night, you could sit on the crescent moon, as if you were swinging in the sky, and touch the shining silver of the stars?

The hidden room was all these things and even more. For in this room, there were two chairs and a table and two pens and many sheets of white paper waiting to be filled with beauty. And it was here, in this hidden room, that I learned the magic and wonder of writing the stories of our lives. I learned that in the world of imagination, anything is possible.

I loved going to the hidden room more than anything in the whole world.

Months went by. One day, as usual, we went to the library. I ran up the stairs and down the hallway and into the children's reading room and over to where the librarian was always standing, waiting to grant us access to the hidden room. But on this day, the librarian was on vacation. There was a substitute librarian and she was frowning.

I stopped dead in my tracks.

Quietly I asked, "May we go into the hidden room?"

"Sit down and behave," she said sharply. "There is no running in the library. And as for this so-called hidden room: I have no idea what you're talking about."

Slowly and with defeat, I walked over to my mother. "Well Mom. We're in a library. We're surrounded by books. All our dreams are supposed to come true. And now look. We can't even get into the hidden room. Now what do we do?"

And this is when my mother told me the secret of the hidden room. The secret changed my life forever.

My mother said, "This not being able to get into the hidden room: this is not a problem. Because, the real hidden room, the most beautiful room in the whole wide world, the room that just gets better and better as you go on in life if you care for it, the most magical room of all: that room is really ...

inside you. And inside me. And inside every single one
of us. This is the magical place where our imagination lives,
and where we go to make up stories and to draw pictures and
to sing the songs of our souls. The real hidden room is the place
inside us where, no matter how sad we might feel, we can rewrite the
ending of our days into something beautiful."

And then my mother said, "I'll tell you what. I know you're still

disappointed that we can't get into the real hidden room, so here's

what we'll do. When we get home today, let's take out all the crayons

from all the cupboards and all the drawers and put them in a huge mountain

in the middle of the living room floor. And the mountain will be so high it will

reach the sky. And when we climb the mountain, we'll be able to touch the

blue of the sky with the palms of our hands. And then let's each take a blank

piece of paper and let's each draw a picture of our hidden room."

And perhaps the hidden room looked like this

20

Or perhaps the hidden room looked like this

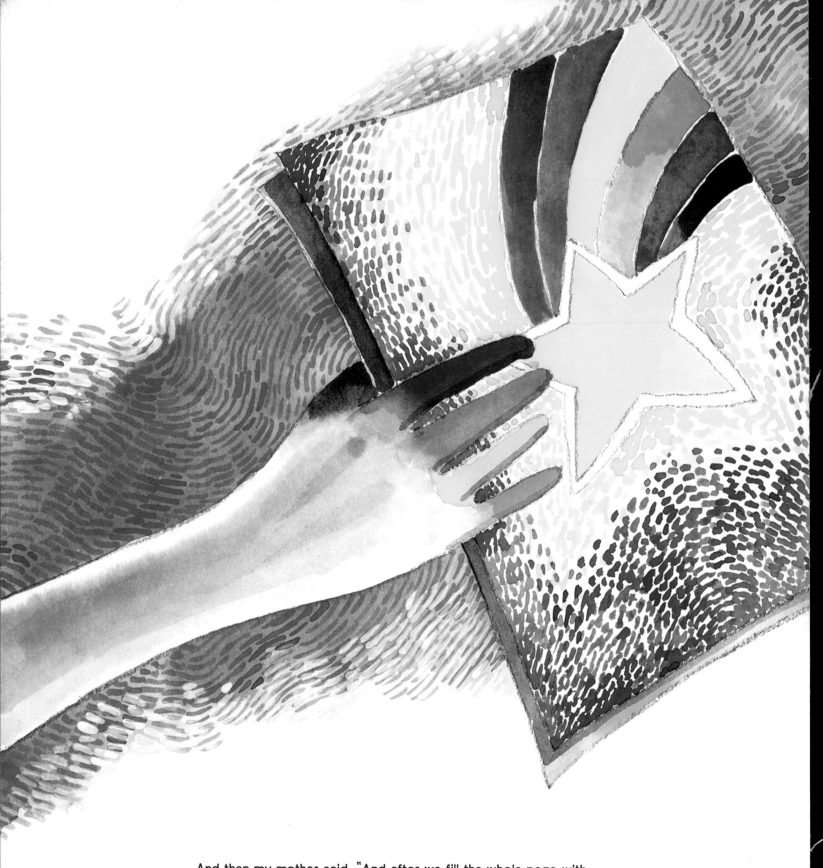

And then my mother said, "And after we fill the whole page with beautiful colors, let's go back to the library and give our drawings to the librarian who wouldn't let us in the hidden room."

And I said, "Wait a minute Mom. That's really not fair. She was crabby and cranky and grumpy and grouchy. Why should we give her anything?"

And my mother said, "Maybe the reason she's crabby and cranky and grumpy and grouchy is, she's forgotten she has a hidden room inside of her. And maybe if we give her a gift, she'll remember."

"Because you see," my mother said,

"In the story of our lives, we're going to color the whole world beautiful.

We're going to leave rainbow trails wherever we go."

The End

(but not really)

Visions from the Hidden Room

When we go into our hidden room, magical things happen. On the following pages are visions we received while in our very special hidden room. The words sometimes came to us unexpected, and often took us by surprise.

We may have set out to write a tribute to the color yellow, but ended up writing a piece called "In Honor of the Color Blue." We may have come out of our hidden room saying with amazement, "I never knew I had that poem, or that character, or that story, inside me." We may have gone into our hidden room feeling like the color of sadness, and then come out feeling like a shimmering rainbow of living light.

We share our visions with the hope that readers and writers everywhere will celebrate the wonder and mystery of their own hidden room, and bring forth the magic within them.

And if anyone feels like writing a tribute to the color yellow, or to any other color, we feel the world will be a more beautiful place for it.

In Honor of the Color Blue

Somewhere deep in the universe there is a swirling energy of blue.

Indigos, cobalts, navys, prussians, oceanics, cornflowers.

Blues with purple, blues with red, blues with green.

Blue-violet and violet-blue. Translucent sheets of blue.

Blue the day and blue the night.

Blue the dust-trailing-comet which traverses the night sky.

Blue of the sky on top of a snow-covered hill the moment before a silent sunset.

Blue of the sky at night when a blue moon floats over a blue ocean reflecting silver-blue.

A wide field of blue spruce trees reaching for a gray-blue sky.

The blue of Matisse and the blue of Monet.

The blue of the stained glass at the front of a dark and empty sanctuary on a sun-filled day.

And suddenly, all the blues become a million shining stars against a velvet spread of the deepest

blue, a place where no man-made light can be found anywhere.

wonder

minutes hold hands with hours

and race through the day

do not lose your sense of wonder

whispered the leaf to the flower

you mean said the flower the way

the moonlight shines in the middle of the night

yes answered the leaf and the way

your fragrance fills the air

oh the flower nodded and the way

you blossom each year

into this beauty   that is spring

because we dreamed it

we dreamed

of a clear blue sky

and horse clouds

racing with beams of sun

we dreamed

of this day

filled with budding trees

and the music of every bird

because we dreamed it

it came true

Rhapsody of the Numbers

The students sit in a classroom studying math.

In the meantime, the shapes on the chalkboard begin to change.

The parallelogram turns itself into a mobile star that won't be still,

each point growing longer and shorter as it shimmers.

The rhomboid turns into a slap-happy Doppelganger

of itself lounging in the sun, smoking a cigar from Cuba

and donning the latest model of Ray Ban sunglasses.

The circles turn themselves into harps which spin and do cartwheels,

and all the numbers on the plain green number line

jump down and begin to boogie down the aisles.

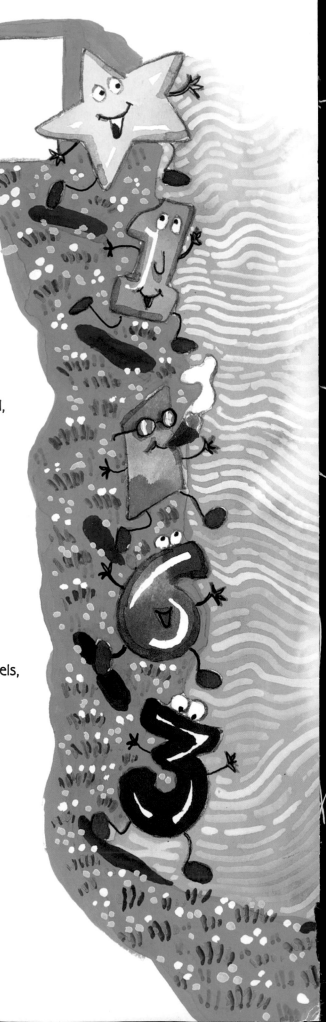

The numbers and shapes form a line and begin marching around the room chanting in an

incantation of pure glee, "One plus one is one! Hey! Three plus three is two! Hey! Nine

plus nine is one! Hey!" and they throw their arms into the air joyfully. The numbers and the

shapes march around the room, throwing out their limbs with each euphoric cry, and they

march to the door that will lead to freedom and kick it down, and march down the hall doing

the cha-cha, singing and chanting; they march by the literature classroom, and shout, "Hey!

Come on!" and the words of the poem leap off the page and join the party, join the troupe

that fox-trots down the hallways of the school, past the classroom of foreign languages,

and the marching numbers and the marching shapes and the marching words of poetry shout,

"Hey! Come on!"

And the words of the foreign languages vault out of the classroom and join the parade, join the revelry, join the locomotion, and the numbers and the shapes and the words march down the hallway, and bang, clang, crash, boom, and out into the street they go, stomping and chanting and yodeling and whooping, singing, "Go tell it on the mountain, over the hills and everywhere!", singing, "Mine eyes have seen the glory of the coming of the Lord!", singing, "And before I'll be a slave, I'll be buried in my grave!" and the numbers become a galaxy the shapes become love the words become salvation, and still they are singing, they are marching, and they cry, "We're marching! For freedom!"

And they march past the tabernacle and the mosque and the temple and the church and invite the words that are the spirit and not the letter to join them, and the words that are the spirit break free from their lexicons and join the gala, join the spree, join the fanfare and flaunt themselves in formations of handsprings and pirouettes and twirls, and the numbers and the shapes and the words march up to the mountain top and they look over Jordan and see everyone in the world embracing each other and saluting each other and clasping hands and shouting for joy. And all the while the numbers and the shapes and the words are harmonizing together, harmonizing like a Mozart symphony, like a Beethoven quartet, like a Bach cantata, like a blue grass band of banjos and fiddles and harmonicas, harmonizing like um-pah bands playing down in New Orleans and opera singers belting it out on the stage of La Scala, all the while dancing like those who dance on the river banks, on the Day of Atonement, on the shores of the Black Sea, on the night when the stars scatter themselves across a pitch black sky, and the sun dances and the moon dances and the earth dances. And so it was, and so it shall be, forevermore: the rhapsody of the numbers.

"Personification squared."

"Make that cubed."

35

unknown land

there are waves

coming endlessly

against the coral reefs

being shelled

with mysteries

that only the sea can know

and the tall hopes

coming bravely

like daring seafarers

to an unknown land

that only you

    can know